I Can't Find my Tooth!

An Ivy and Mack story

Written by Rebecca Colby

Illustrated by Gustavo Mazali

Collins

Who's in this story?

Listen and say

Ms Snow

Alex

Mack

Download the audio at www.collins.co.uk/839690

the cook

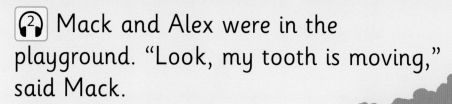 Mack and Alex were in the playground. "Look, my tooth is moving," said Mack.

"What tooth?" said Alex.

4

Mack put his finger in his mouth.
"My tooth! It's not there!" he said.

"Oh no," Mack looked at his tummy.
"Alex, I think my tooth is in here!"

"Don't be silly," said Alex. "You can't eat your tooth."

"Then where is it?" asked Mack.

"I can't see it!" said Alex.

"It was in my mouth this morning!" said Mack. "I cleaned my teeth and it moved."

"What about in our Maths lesson?" said Alex.

"Yes." said Mack.

Alex had an idea. "What about when you had lunch?"

"Oh ... I don't know ..." said Mack.

Mack asked the cook. "Hello! I can't find my tooth. Is it here?"

"Oh, dear!" said the cook. "I'm sorry, Mack. Your tooth isn't here."

The boys looked for Mack's tooth in the classroom. They looked under the tables. They looked under the chairs. But no tooth!

Then they looked under the coats. And under the bags. But no tooth!

"Let's look in the bathroom," said Mack.

"It's not in here," said Alex. "Where can we look now?"

"I think it's in my tummy," said Mack.

"I've got one more idea," said Alex.

The boys looked in the grass.
But no tooth!

"Hello!" said a girl. It was Ivy. "What are you doing?" she asked.

"I think my tooth is in my tummy," said Mack.

"*Hmmm ...*" said Ivy.

"Oh, Mack," said Ivy. "I don't think your tooth is in your tummy. I think I know where it is. Come with me."

Ivy got Mack's lunch bag. "Look in here," she said.

Mack opened the bag. Alex picked up Mack's apple. There was his tooth!

"Ivy is very clever," said Alex.

"Yes, she is," said Mack. "Ivy always helps me."

"I haven't got a big sister," said Alex.

Alex pointed and asked, "What's that?"

"It's my new tooth. Ivy told me!"
said Mack.

"She knows everything," said Alex.

Mack showed Ms Snow his tooth.
Ms Snow gave Mack a star.

"Do old people grow new teeth?"
asked Mack.

"No," said Ms Snow. "Only children.
Oh, and crocodiles!"

That night, Ivy said, "Put your tooth under your pillow, Mack."

"Why?" asked Mack. "Does Croc want it?"

"Look under there in the morning," said Ivy.

"Ivy, are you my 'tooth-sister'?" asked Mack.

"Yes, I am." Ivy smiled and went to bed.

21

Picture dictionary

finger

mouth

teeth

tooth

tummy

1 Look and order the story

2 Listen and say

Collins

Published by Collins
An imprint of HarperCollins*Publishers*
Westerhill Road
Bishopbriggs
Glasgow
G64 2QT

HarperCollins*Publishers*
1st Floor, Watermarque Building
Ringsend Road
Dublin 4
Ireland

William Collins' dream of knowledge for all began with the publication of his first book in 1819.

A self-educated mill worker, he not only enriched millions of lives, but also founded a flourishing publishing house. Today, staying true to this spirit, Collins books are packed with inspiration, innovation and practical expertise. They place you at the centre of a world of possibility and give you exactly what you need to explore it.

© HarperCollins*Publishers* Limited 2020

10 9 8 7 6 5 4 3 2

ISBN 978-0-00-839690-9

Collins® and COBUILD® are registered trademarks of HarperCollins*Publishers* Limited

www.collins.co.uk/elt

British Library Cataloguing in Publication Data

A catalogue record for this publication is available from the British Library.

Author: Rebecca Colby
Illustrator: Gustavo Mazali (Beehive)
Series editor: Rebecca Adlard
Publishing manager: Lisa Todd
Product managers: Jennifer Hall and Caroline Green
In-house editor: Alma Puts Keren
Project manager: Emily Hooton
Editor: Deborah Friedland
Proofreaders: Natalie Murray and Michael Lamb
Cover designer: Kevin Robbins
Typesetter: 2Hoots Publishing Services Ltd
Audio produced by id audio, London
Reading guide author: Julie Penn
Production controller: Rachel Weaver
Printed and bound by: GPS Group, Slovenia

Download the audio for this book and a reading guide for parents and teachers at www.collins.co.uk/839690